P9-APM-281

Once Upon a Timeless Tale

Little Red Riding Hood

Story by Charles Perrault
Retold by Margrete Lamond

Pictures by
Anna Pignataro

Little Hare
www.littleharebooks.com

nce upon a time—in the days when wolves could talk and should have known better—there lived a little girl. She was as pretty as the freckles on her nose, and as good as could be, except when she wasn't.

She had a mother at home and, in the next village, on the other side of a deep dark wood, she had a grandmother. This grandmother loved her so dearly she had already given her everything she could think of, and more besides. One of her gifts was a bright red cloak with a hood, and the little girl thought it so handsome she wore it all day, from morning till night and even to bed. That was why everyone called her Red Riding Hood.

One day Red Riding Hood's mother said, 'Go and see how your grandmother is doing, for I hear she is too ill to get out of bed. Take her a cake, and this little pot of butter. And mind you don't dawdle along the way.'

Red Riding Hood promised and set out immediately along the path to her grandmother's house. The path twisted and turned through the deep dark wood and, as Red Riding Hood rounded a bend, she suddenly came face to face with a wolf.

This wolf looked very much as though he might like to eat her on the spot. But there were woodcutters working nearby who would hear her scream, so he didn't.

Instead he bowed politely.

'Good day to you, Red Riding Hood,' he said.

'Thank you, Mr Wolf,' she replied.

'Where are you off to, so early in the morning?'

'I'm off to visit my grandmother.'

'And what's that you've got in your basket?'

'Cake and a little pot of butter,' said Red Riding Hood. 'Grandmother is too ill to get out of bed, and the cake should give her strength.'

'I see,' said the wolf. 'I wouldn't mind a little cake and butter myself. And just where does your grandmother live, if you don't mind telling me?'

‘On the other side of the wood,’ said Red Riding Hood, who didn’t mind at all. ‘Past the mill, over the stream, under the three oak trees and beside the hazel hedge. It is easy to find.’

‘Easy to find, indeed,’ the wolf agreed. ‘But why don’t you wander in the woods with your cake and butter, instead of following this dull old path? Look at those bluebells and violets blossoming amongst the trees! Listen to those wrens twittering amongst the leaves! You will still find your way to your grandmother’s house.’

Little Red Riding Hood saw the violets and bluebells peeping through the moss.

She heard the birds twittering on their twigs.

'I could pick a bunch of violets for my grandmother,' she thought to herself. 'And the wolf is right: I'll reach the village just as easily through the wood as I would by following the path.'

So she ran off into the woods with her cake and butter and started to pick violets. Each time she picked one, she saw one even more lovely a little way off, and each time she ran after a flower, she ran deeper into the woods.

But the wolf ran along the path—past the mill, over the stream, under the three oak trees and beside the hazel hedge—straight to the grandmother's house.

It certainly was easy to find.

He knocked on the door.

'Who's there?' cried a voice.

'Red Riding Hood,' piped the wolf. 'I've brought you cake and a little pot of butter.'

'Just pull the bobbin to lift the latch,' the grandmother called out. 'I'm too ill to get out of bed.'

The wolf pulled the bobbin and lifted the latch, and the door swung open. He went straight to the grandmother in her bed and swallowed her whole, shawl and all. Then he took some clothes out of her clothes chest, put them on, stuck one of her caps on his head and climbed into her bed.

When Red Riding Hood finally arrived at her grandmother's house, she saw that the door was off the latch.

'Hello?' she called.

But there was no answer.

She crept inside, went to the bed and drew back the curtains. There lay her grandmother, with her cap drawn down to her eyes, looking quite peculiar.

'Goodness, Granny, what big ears you have!' she cried.

'All the better to hear you with, my dear,' croaked the wolf.

Red Riding Hood wondered at her grandmother's hoarse voice.

She thought her grandmother must be very ill indeed. ‘But, Granny,’ she said, ‘what big eyes you have!’

‘All the better to see you with, my dear,’ whispered the wolf.

‘But, goodness, Granny, what big hands you have!’

‘All the better to hold you with!’ growled the wolf. He was beginning to feel impatient with all the chatter.

‘But, goodness gracious, Granny, what big teeth you have!’

‘All the better to eat you with!’ roared the wolf. And he jumped out of bed, grabbed Red Riding Hood, and swallowed her whole.

Then he climbed back into bed, fell asleep and was soon snoring fit to make the windows rattle.

Well, it wasn't long before a woodsman passed by on his way home to dinner. He heard those windows rattling, and then he heard the snoring, and he thought to himself that the snoring was far too loud. As the door was still off the latch, he went in and there, on the bed, lay the wolf. He was still wearing the grandmother's clothes, and his belly was bigger than a prize pumpkin and tight as a drum.

It didn't take the woodsman long to work out what had happened.

'The wolf has eaten the old lady!' he said. Straightaway he took a pair of scissors and cut open the wolf.

Out jumped Red Riding Hood. 'Oh, how horrible that was!' she cried.

Next the grandmother was pulled out but she had little to say because she was almost dead with fright.

'Fetch some rocks,' said the woodsman.

Red Riding Hood wasted no time and fetched a load of stones. Then she helped the woodsman fill the wolf's belly with them.

The wolf woke up and saw them glaring at him. His first thought was to run away.

But the stones made him terribly thirsty, so he staggered outside to the well in search of a drink. No sooner did he lean over the edge of the well than the stones in his belly made him fall in, and he drowned.

Red Riding Hood, the grandmother and the woodsman shared the cake and butter, and they soon felt much better.

'That should teach you,' said the grandmother, 'not to talk to wolves.'

'It should teach the wolf,' said Red Riding Hood, 'not to talk to little girls.'

And once they had agreed on this, everyone lived happily ever after.

Little Hare Books
an imprint of
Hardie Grant Egmont
Ground Floor, Building 1, 658 Church Street
Richmond, Victoria 3121, Australia

www.littleharebooks.com

Text by Margrete Lamond

First published 2014

Cataloguing-in-Publication details are available from the
National Library of Australia

978 1 921894 87 9 (hbk.)

Designed by Vida & Luke Kelly
Produced by Pica Digital, Singapore
Printed in China by Wai Man Book Binding Ltd.

5 4 3 2 1